Words to Know Befo

clothes

eighth

excited

opened

shelf

someone

thought

www.rourkeeducationalmedia.com

Edited by Luana K. Mitten
Illustrated by Anita DuFalla
Art Direction and Page Layout by Renee Brady

Library of Congress Cataloging-in-Publication Data

Cleland, Jo
 Best Birthday / Jo Cleland.
     p. cm. -- (Little Birdie Books)
 ISBN 978-1-61741-798-6 (hard cover) (alk. paper)
 ISBN 978-1-61236-002-7 (soft cover)
 Library of Congress Control Number: 2011924608

Printed in China, FOFO I - Production Company
  Shenzhen, Guangdong Province

rourkeeducationalmedia.com

customerservice@rourkeeducationalmedia.com • PO Box 643328 Vero Beach, Florida 32964

Best Birthday

By Jo Cleland

Illustrated by Anita DuFalla

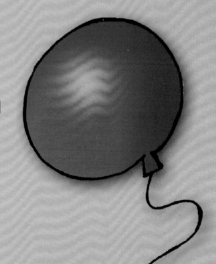

4

Mia was excited. It was her birthday.

She looked at the seven dolls on her shelf.

"Today there will be eight," she thought.

But when she looked at her gifts, she didn't see one from Grandma.

Mia opened a craft box from Sis, a game from Will, and clothes from Mom and Dad. She smiled. "Thanks!"

Then Mia asked, "Did anything come from Grandma?"

Will said, "Maybe she thinks you're too old for dolls."

14

Mom said, "Let's go. Your dad is meeting us at Pizza Pete's for your birthday dinner."

On the way, Mia couldn't stop thinking about the empty spot on her shelf.

Someone was sitting with dad at the table. "Grandma!" Mia shouted.

After hugs, Grandma opened her bag. She said, "Happy Birthday," and handed Mia her eighth doll.

After Reading Activities

You and the Story...

Why do you think Mia knew her grandmother was going to give her a doll for her birthday?

How do you think Mia was feeling when she did not see a gift from her grandmother?

Do you have a favorite birthday gift?

Words You Know Now...

Some of the words below have the *es* or *ed* ending. On a piece of paper, write a sentence for each word that has an *es* or *ed* ending.

clothes	shelf
eighth	someone
excited	thought
opened	

You Could...Plan Your Next Birthday Party

- Use a calendar to find out how many days until your birthday.

- Make invitations for your birthday. Make sure the invitations tell:
    - What the party is for
    - The date and time of the party
    - Where the party will be held

- Plan what you will do at the party.

- Make a list of what supplies you need for the party.

About the Author

Jo Cleland enjoys writing books, composing songs, and making games. She is a grandma who loves to give birthday presents.

About the Illustrator

Acclaimed for its versatility in style, Anita DuFalla's work has appeared in many educational books, newspaper articles, and business advertisements and on numerous posters, book and magazine covers, and even giftwraps. Anita's passion for pattern is evident in both her artwork and her collection of 400 patterned tights. She lives in the Friendship neighborhood of Pittsburgh, Pennsylvania with her son, Lucas.